POKéMON™

Attack of the Prehistoric Pokémon

TYLERT

POKÉMON™

Attack of the Prehistoric Pokémon

Adapted by Tracey West

SCHOLASTIC INC.
New York   Toronto   London   Auckland   Sydney
Mexico City   New Delhi   Hong Kong

ISBN 0-439-13550-8

12   11   10   9   8   7   6   5   9/9   0   1   2   3   4/0

Printed in the U.S.A.

First Scholastic printing, September 1999

The World of Pokémon

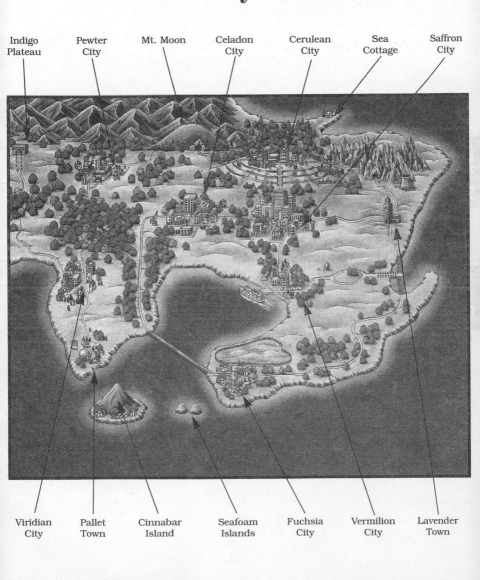

Indigo Plateau

Pewter City

Mt. Moon

Celadon City

Cerulean City

Sea Cottage

Saffron City

Viridian City

Pallet Town

Cinnabar Island

Seafoam Islands

Fuchsia City

Vermilion City

Lavender Town

The Great Fossil Rush

"We've been walking for weeks," Ash Ketchum complained. He looked around. Dry reddish sand covered the ground. Tall, jagged rock peaks dotted the landscape. "Why did we come all the way out here, anyway?"

Ash's friend Misty laughed. "Ash, for someone who wants to become the world's greatest Pokémon master, you sure do complain a lot."

Ash Ketchum, the world's greatest Pokémon master. That was Ash's dream.

Ever since he turned ten, he had been traveling around the country searching for Pokémon, creatures with amazing powers. Ash knew catching and training Pokémon could be a real challenge. He knew he shouldn't complain. Still . . .

"But to be a Pokémon master, I need to battle my Pokémon against the Pokémon of other trainers," Ash protested. "How will we find any trainers to battle out here, in the middle of nowhere?"

Ash's friend Brock shook his head. Brock was older than Ash and more experienced at training Pokémon.

"Ash, there are Pokémon trainers everywhere," Brock said. "Besides, if you really want to be a Pokémon master, you should be thinking about raising strong, healthy Pokémon. You'll need powerful Pokémon to battle the other trainers in the Pokémon League Tournament. Winning the tournament is the only way you'll ever become the world's greatest Pokémon master."

"Yeah Ash," Misty agreed. She looked into the distance. "Hey, maybe we'll even find some rare Pokémon out here."

"I guess you're right," Ash said. He climbed up on a smooth, flat rock. "But let's take a break, okay? I'm thirsty."

"Pika!"

It was Pikachu. Ash looked down at the lightning mouse Pokémon. Pikachu was bright yellow, with pointy ears and a tail shaped like a lightning bolt. Pikachu was Ash's very first Pokémon. It went everywhere with Ash.

Ash picked up Pikachu. "I guess you're thirsty, too, Pikachu."

Pikachu nodded. *"Pika."*

Ash took off his red-and-white baseball cap and ran his hand through his dark hair. Then he opened up his knapsack and

took out a bottle of water.

Misty leaned against the rock. Her red hair gleamed in the bright sun.

"It sure is beautiful here," she said.

"I guess it is," Ash admitted. "Where are we, anyway?"

"We're in Grandpa Canyon," Brock said. "It's one of the world's natural wonders."

"I *wonder* what we'll find here," Ash joked.

Misty straightened up. She pointed ahead. "Looks like we're going to find more than we expected," she said.

Ash turned. A huge crowd of people was hiking down the rocky trail in front of them. They carried shovels and picks. They were heading down to the bottom of the canyon.

"I wonder what's up?" Ash asked. He ran up to a man at the head of the crowd. He was an older man, with a bald head and a large gray mustache.

"What's everybody doing here?" Ash asked.

The man looked through his glasses at Ash. "Why, haven't you heard?" he said. "It's the Great Fossil Rush! I'm heading a group of scientists. We believe that rare Pokémon fossils are buried in the canyon."

Misty, Brock, and Pikachu caught up to Ash.

"This is great!" Ash said. "I know I'll find a rare Pokémon fossil. I'll be famous!"

Brock frowned. "I don't like the idea of digging up old Pokémon fossils," he said. "Especially after they've been resting in the earth for such a long time."

"If they've been lying underground for thousands of years, maybe they'd like a little fresh air," Misty said.

Ash hoisted his knapsack on his shoulders and put his hat back on. "You guys can spend all day arguing if you want. I've got a rare fossil to find!"

Ash hurried down the trail with Pikachu beside him. Misty and Brock followed along behind.

"What's the rush, Ash?" Misty asked.

"Don't you see?" Ash said. "This is my big chance to do something special. Until now, Gary Oak has beaten me at every turn."

"He sure has," Misty said.

It was true. Gary was Ash's biggest rival. They had both gotten their Pokémon trainer's license on the same day. Since then, Gary had gone out of his way to try to do everything better than Ash.

Ash continued. "If I find a rare Pokémon fossil, I'll finally *beat him* at something."

Misty cringed. "Maybe not."

Ash was puzzled. "Huh?"

A nasal voice answered him. "Well, if it isn't Ash, the loser. I see you're late, as usual."

Ash spun around.

It was Gary!

Gary was dressed like an explorer, in boots and a brown jacket. There was a leather bag attached to his belt. A wide-brimmed hat covered his brown hair.

The group of cheerleaders who always followed Gary around called out, "Gary! Gary! He's our man! If he can't do it, no one can!"

"That's right," Gary said, sneering. "No one can do it like I can. And guess what? I've already done it."

Ash's heart sank. "What do you mean?"

Gary reached into his bag. He pulled out a chunky gray lump and held it high in the air.

"I've done it!" Gary cried. "I've found the first Pokémon fossil!"

2

Stop That Fuse!

"Hooray, Gary! Hooray, Gary!" The cheerleaders jumped up and down.

Ash looked down and kicked a rock.

"It looks like Gary beat you again," Misty said.

The scientist that Ash had spoken to approached Gary. Gary shoved the fossil into his hand.

"I found it on my very first try," Gary bragged. "I think it's a fossilized Pokémon brain."

The scientist examined the gray lump

carefully. He cleared his throat. "This *is* a fossil," the scientist said. "It's fossilized Pokémon manure!"

The cheerleaders groaned. Gary grinned sheepishly.

Ash laughed.

Gary glared at him. "What are you laughing about, loser? At least I found something!"

Ash turned to Misty and Brock. "Gary's right. If I'm going to find a fossil, I'd better start looking." He grabbed a shovel.

Brock looked around. The canyon was crowded with fossil hunters. "There's no place left to dig here," he said. "Maybe we should find another spot."

"Good idea!" Ash said. He started up the dusty trail.

Misty, Brock, and Pikachu followed Ash up the canyon. Soon they came to a flat patch of land. A large rock jutted out in front of them.

"This looks like the perfect spot to find a fossil," Ash said.

"*Pika!*" Pikachu agreed.

Suddenly, a familiar voice rang in the air.

"*Meowth!* What's taking those guys so long?"

The voice was coming from behind the rock. Ash and his friends tiptoed over to the rock and looked around it. There was Meowth, the talking, catlike Pokémon that belonged to Team Rocket — the most notorious pair of Pokémon thieves in the world.

Ash and the others remained hidden as a red-haired teenage girl and a purple-

haired teenage boy climbed up on a rock in front of Meowth. It was Jessie and James — Team Rocket!

Jessie and James began the Team Rocket motto:

"To protect the world from devastation.
To unite all peoples within our nation.
To denounce the evils of truth and love.
To extend our reach to the stars above.
Jessie!
James!
Team Rocket! Blast off at the speed of light!
Surrender now or prepare to fight!"

"*Meowth!* That's right," Meowth added and then turned to Jessie and James. "But where have you been?" Meowth asked. "Did you plant the dynamite yet?"

James sneered. "Of course we did. Soon we'll blast Grandpa Canyon into smithereens . . ."

". . . and we'll be able to scoop up all those Poké fossils!" Jessie finished.

Ash gasped. "They're going to blow up this whole canyon!"

"All of the people digging here will get caught in the blast," Brock said.

"Pikachu and I will stop them," Ash said. "You two go tell everyone to run for it!"

Misty nodded. "Let's go!"

Misty and Brock ran back down the canyon. Ash scrambled over the rock.

James was holding onto a long fuse. Meowth held a flame to the end of it.

If Meowth lit that fuse, then the dynamite would blast the canyon to pieces!

"Stop right there!" Ash yelled.

James rolled his eyes. "Oh, it's that pest again."

"Always messing up our plans!" Jessie said.

"But this time you're too late!" Meowth said. It lit the fuse. The bright orange flame began to speed toward the dynamite.

Ash knew there was no time to lose. He pulled a Poké Ball from his belt.

"Squirtle, I choose you!" Ash threw the ball.

A Pokémon that looked like a turtle appeared in a blaze of light.

"*Squirtle squirt*," it said.

"Squirtle, squirt out that fuse!" Ash ordered.

Squirtle shot a jet of water from its mouth. The water missed.

"After it, Squirtle!" Ash yelled.

Squirtle chased the fuse down the trail. The Water Pokémon kept squirting water at the flame, but the flame was traveling too fast for Squirtle to catch it.

Ash and Pikachu raced behind Squirtle. Team Rocket and Meowth raced behind them all.

"We can't let that pest stop us," James said.

Jessie threw a Poké Ball. "Arbok! Get them!"

A large, snakelike Pokémon appeared

and began sliding down the trail.

James threw a Poké Ball. "Weezing! Sludge Attack!"

A Poison Pokémon that looked like a purple cloud with two heads appeared. It floated after Ash, Pikachu, and Squirtle.

Squirtle was trying its best to squirt out the fuse. But the flame was too fast.

Ash looked behind him. Team Rocket and their Pokémon were gaining on them.

"We've got you now," James said smugly. "Team Rocket wins —"

James tripped over a rock. He went sprawling into Jessie, Meowth, Arbok, and Weezing. The Pokémon poachers began to roll down the trail. They were out of control.

Slam! Team Rocket crashed into Squirtle, Ash, and Pikachu. They all rolled down the trail. They crashed into a heap.

Ash's head hurt. He looked up. They were in front of a cave.

A cave full of dynamite!

The fuse led to the dynamite. The flame was working its way down the fuse. It was almost there. In a few seconds, the dynamite would explode.

And they would be caught right in the middle!

"Pikachu."

Ash turned his head. Pikachu was standing up. It faced the fuse. Tiny electric sparks were shooting from its body. Pikachu was smiling.

What's Pikachu smiling about? Ash wondered. Then, suddenly, he knew. Pikachu was going to try to stop the fuse.

"Pikachu, no!" Ash cried. "You'll blow up the dynamite!"

"Pika!"

It was too late. Pikachu aimed a bolt of electricity right at the burning fuse.

The electric blast hit the bundle of dynamite.

"Noooooooo!" Ash cried.

The next thing he heard was a deafening roar as the cave exploded in a blast of angry yellow flames.

3

Trapped!

The explosion rocked the canyon. The ground shook.

Ash grabbed Pikachu. Above them, giant rocks tumbled down the canyon walls.

Crack! An earsplitting roar drowned out the sound of the speeding rocks. Ash watched in horror as the ground below them split open like an eggshell.

"Hold on tight, Pikachu!" Ash yelled. He held his Pokémon tightly.

Suddenly, Ash felt himself falling down,

down through the crack in the earth. He landed on the ground below with a thud.

Then his world went black.

Above him, Misty and Brock raced to the site of the explosion.

"We're too late!" Misty cried.

Misty and Brock looked at the giant pile of rocks on the canyon floor.

"The explosion must have caused a rock slide," Brock said.

"I can see that," Misty said. "But where are Ash and Team Rocket?"

Brock frowned and looked at the rocks. "They must have been . . . buried."

"Then let's start digging!" Misty cried.

Misty and Brock began pushing the heavy rocks out of the way. Suddenly, they heard a faint coughing sound. A small head pushed through the rocks. It was Squirtle. The Water Pokémon was covered with dirt.

"Squirtle!" Misty cried. "Are you all right?"

"Squirtle," the Pokémon replied. *"Squirtle, squirtle, squirtle!"*

Misty understood that Squirtle was trying to say, "Ash and the others fell through a hole in the canyon floor! The rocks are blocking the hole. It's their only way out."

"We've got to get help!" Brock said.

"I'll go," Misty said. "You and Squirtle keep digging!"

Misty raced back up the trail.

A round pink Pokémon with big blue eyes popped out from behind a rock.

Misty stopped. "Jigglypuff!" she cried. "What are you doing here?"

The Pokémon held out a small microphone.

"I know you want to sing us your song, Jigglypuff," Misty said. "But I'm in a hurry right now."

Jigglypuff frowned.

"Sorry, Jigglypuff," Misty said. "But I've got to get help for Ash and Pikachu — before it's too late!"

4

The Prehistoric Pokémon

Ash opened his eyes. He slowly sat up.

Pikachu was next to him. It looked dazed but not hurt. Team Rocket and their Pokémon were a few feet away. It looked like they were knocked out.

Ash looked around. They were in some kind of cavern. The rocky walls were bluish-black. Water slowly dripped from the ceiling. Stalactites hung from the roof like icicles.

James sat up. "Where are we?" he asked groggily.

Jessie opened her eyes. "It looks like we're in the center of the earth!" she replied.

Meowth leaped to its feet, panicked. "This is a cave!" it cried. "The dynamite must have blown a hole in the roof, and we fell in! We must be buried deep under the earth's crust!"

James turned to Ash. "This is all your fault, you twcrp!"

Jessie glared at him. "If you hadn't tried to blow out that fuse, we wouldn't be here."

Ash and Pikachu jumped up. "You guys

are the ones who planted all that dynamite in the first place!" Ash said angrily.

"*Pika!*" Pikachu was angry, too.

"*Meowth*! It doesn't matter how we got here," Meowth said. "All that matters is getting out. Look!" The Pokémon pointed up.

Ash looked up at the roof of the cave. Rocks covered the hole that they had fallen through.

"The hole is blocked!" Ash said. "We're trapped!"

James sobbed. Tears flowed from his eyes. "We're doomed! We're all doomed."

Jessie shook James. "Quit it. There's got to be some way out of here."

"*Pika.*" Pikachu was pointing to a dark corner of the cave.

"What is it, Pikachu?" Ash asked. "Did you find a way out?"

Pikachu shook its head. It kept pointing.

Ash squinted into the darkness. Then he gasped. He saw what Pikachu saw.

Eyes. Glowing red eyes.

"W-what's that?" James asked.

Four Pokémon stepped out of the blackness.

Ash had never seen them before. He took out Dexter, his Pokédex. Dexter was a handheld computer that stored information about all Pokémon.

"Dexter, what are they?" Ash asked.

One Pokémon had a curved shell, like a snail. Two eyes and blue tentacles protruded from the shell's mouth. "That is Omanyte," Dexter said.

The second Pokémon looked like Omanyte, but its shell was covered with sharp spikes. It also had a round mouth with sharp pincers. "That is Omastar, the evolved form of Omanyte," Dexter said.

The third Pokémon had a flat, smooth shell, kind of like a horseshoe crab. Two red eyes glowed from beneath the shell. "That is Kabuto," Dexter said.

The fourth Pokémon was the scariest-looking of all. It stood on two legs. Its long arms were curved like swords. Its body was covered in hard gray armor. "That is Kabutops, the evolved form of Kabuto," Dexter said.

Dexter continued. "It is believed these Pokémon became extinct tens of thousands of years ago. The details of their behavior are shrouded in mystery. None of these Pokémon have ever been seen alive."

Jessie and James jumped up and down. "Rare Pokémon! We're going to be rich!" they cried.

Ash eyed the prehistoric Pokémon nervously. "Uh, these Pokémon don't seem as happy as you guys do!" he said.

The Pokémon were making low, growling

sounds. Their eyes glowed fiercely in the darkness.

"They look like they just woke up," Jessie said. "Maybe these Pokémon weren't fossilized — they were just sleeping!"

"That's it!" James said. "The dynamite must have woken them up after thousands of years."

"Let's stop talking," Jessie said, "and start capturing!"

Jessie took a Poké Ball off her belt and threw it at Kabutops.

Kabutops swiped at the Poké Ball with its long, curved arms. It sent the ball flying back through the air. The ball hit Meowth on the head.

"Uh-oh," James said.

The prehistoric Pokémon growled and took a step forward. Then another. Omanyte, Omastar, Kabuto, and Kabutops emerged from the depths of the cave. The eight Pokémon advanced on Ash and Team Rocket.

Ash turned to run. There was nowhere to go.

The prehistoric Pokémon had them cornered.

"We're trapped!" Jessie cried.

5

Battle in the cavern

"We have to battle!" Ash cried. He pulled a Poké Ball from his belt. "Charmeleon, I choose you!"

An orange-red Fire Pokémon burst from the ball. With its flaming tail, Charmeleon was powerful. Ash had evolved it from a Charmander.

"Charmeleon, use your flame to stop them!" Ash commanded.

Charmeleon looked at Ash and rolled its eyes. It sat down.

"It *still* won't obey me!" Ash cried. Ash

knew that high-level Pokémon like Charmeleon would only obey trainers with lots of experience. He kept hoping that Charmeleon would do what he asked — especially now, when he really needed it.

Ash reached for another Poké Ball, but it was too late. The prehistoric Pokémon were right on top of them. Jessie, James, Meowth, Arbok, and Weezing were already making their escape. Ash dodged the sharp arms of Kabutops and dashed down a passageway in the cavern. Pikachu was at his heels.

Behind them, Omastar began to spin wildly in the air. The Pokémon charged after them. Ash felt Omastar's hard shell crash into his back. The force sent him sprawling into Jessie, James, and Meowth. They all crashed to the floor with a thud.

Arbok and Weezing continued to run from the prehistoric Pokémon.

"Arbok! Weezing! Stop running away!" Jessie called out.

"Yes, attack!" James commanded.

Arbok and Weezing stopped. The prehistoric Pokémon descended on them and bit them with their sharp pincers.

"Pika!"

Ash jumped up. One of the Kabutops was advancing on Pikachu.

"Pikachu! Give it your electric shock!" Ash ordered.

Pikachu's tiny yellow body began to shake. Sparks flew from its pointy ears.

"Pikachu!"

Pikachu hurled a bolt of electricity at Kabutops. It was a hit!

Kabutops brushed off the charge like it was nothing.

Kabutops swiped at Pikachu with its sharp arms. Pikachu jumped into Ash's arms just in time.

"Electricity won't work against these guys," Ash said. "Charmeleon, attack!"

Charmeleon was napping on a rock. It completely ignored Ash's command.

"Not again!" Ash cried.

"Pika, pika!" Pikachu screamed.

Ash spun around.

Two Kabutops flew at them.

Ash and Pikachu were pinned against the wall of the cave. There was nowhere to run.

They were trapped!

Ash and Pikachu closed their eyes and braced for the attack.

Suddenly, the two Kabutops stopped in their tracks.

Omanyte and Omastar stopped, too.

A strange, whooshing sound filled the cave.

The prehistoric Pokémon scattered quickly.

"What's going on?" Ash wondered.

"It's a miracle!" Jessie cried.

"We're alive!" said James happily.

Meowth frowned. "I hear something else. . . ."

The whooshing sound grew louder. Ash looked in the direction of the noise.

A large Pokémon was flying through the cavern. The Pokémon had leathery gray wings. Its jaws were opened wide to reveal rows of sharp teeth.

"It's coming right for us!" Ash yelled.

6

Aerodactyl Attack!

Above the cave, Brock, Misty, and the other fossil hunters were frantically trying to move the rocks from the hole.

A police officer named Jenny was leading the effort.

"Keep tossing those rocks aside," Jenny ordered. "We're almost there."

Misty looked at the heavy boulders on the rock pile. "We'll never move these ourselves," she said.

Brock took out a Poké Ball. "I know what to do."

Brock threw the ball. "Geodude, go!"

A Rock Pokémon appeared. Geodude was a gray Pokémon that looked like a round boulder. It had two strong arms.

"Geodude! Help us move this pile of rocks!" Brock commanded.

Geodude began lifting up the heavy rocks and tossing them aside.

Misty felt a little better.

"You'd better hold on, Ash," she said softly. "We're almost there!"

Underneath them, the flying Pokémon began its attack. It swooped down at Charmeleon and slashed at it with its sharp claws. It sent Charmeleon sprawling off the rock.

The flying Pokémon perched on the rock. It sniffed the air in the cave with its long snout.

Ash, Pikachu, and Team Rocket hid behind another rock. Ash took out his Pokédex.

"Aerodactyl is an extinct flying Pokémon," Dexter said. "Its hard fangs and sharp claws suggest that it was a carnivore."

"What's a carnivore?" Ash asked.

James turned pale. "That means it thinks we're dinner!"

"That must be why the others ran away!" Jessie said.

Meowth gulped. "I hope it doesn't like *cat* food!"

Aerodactyl heard them. It flew off its perch and aimed right for them.

"Run!" James cried.

Ash and Pikachu followed Team Rocket

down a corridor in the cave. Ash looked behind him.

Charmeleon was on its feet. It looked angry. It faced Aerodactyl.

"It looks like Charmeleon's ready to fight!" Ash said.

Aerodactyl flew at Charmeleon. Before the Fire Pokémon could attack, Aerodactyl knocked Charmeleon to the ground.

Ash cringed. "A first-round knockout."

"Let's go back to my first plan," James said. "Run!"

Ash and the others ran down the corridor. The whooshing sound of Aerodactyl's wings was right behind them.

Suddenly, a bright light blinded Ash. He looked up.

It was the hole in the cave. Some of the rocks were gone. There was a way out!

Misty peered down into the hole.

"Ash! Are you there?" she called.

"Get us out of here!" Ash cried. "And hurry —"

Ash felt a sharp claw on his back.

It was Aerodactyl!

The flying Pokémon picked up Ash in its claws.

Aerodactyl flew up to the hole. Pikachu and Charmeleon grabbed onto its tail. Aerodactyl burst through the loosened rocks.

The force sent Pikachu and Charmeleon sprawling to the ground.

Ash was still in Aerodactyl's grasp.

"Help!" Ash cried.

Pikachu ran up to Misty and Brock. *"Pikachu!"* it cried urgently. *"Pikachu!"*

Misty grabbed Brock's arm. "We've got to save Ash," she said, "before he becomes that Pokémon's dinner!"

7

Charizard vs. Aerodactyl

Aerodactyl flew high up above the canyon floor and landed on a tall, rocky peak. It wouldn't release Ash from its claws.

"Somebody get me down!" Ash called out.

Misty looked at Brock. "What should we do?"

"*Jiggly,*" said a small voice.

Misty and Brock spun around. It was Jigglypuff, the singing Pokémon.

"You're still here," Misty said. "Do you still want to sing your song?"

45

Jigglypuff nodded.

"That's it!" Misty said. "I'll get Jigglypuff to sing its slumber song."

"Its slumber song?" asked Brock. "You know what happens when Jigglypuff sings that song. Everyone who hears it falls asleep! We can't help Ash if we're asleep."

"But Aerodactyl will fall asleep, too!" Misty said. "Then Ash will be safe."

"Good idea!" Brock agreed.

Misty turned to Jigglypuff. "If you help us out now," she said, "later we'll listen to your song as much as you want."

Jigglypuff smiled.

"Hey, look at Charmeleon," Brock said.

The Fire Pokémon was staring up at Aerodactyl. It stomped its feet on the ground. It let out an angry roar.

From his rocky perch, Ash watched as a bright yellow fire exploded around Charmeleon. The fire faded.

Charmeleon was gone. In its place was a large flying Pokémon with huge wings and a flaming tail.

A Charizard!

Ash couldn't believe it. "Charmeleon has evolved into Charizard!"

Charizard spit a stream of red flame from its mouth. It looked up at Aerodactyl.

The prehistoric Pokémon's jaws were wide open. Drool dripped from its long pink tongue. It stared hungrily at Ash.

"It's going to take a bite out of Ash!" Misty cried.

Charizard roared again. It used its new wings to fly up to Aerodactyl.

Aerodactyl saw Charizard from the corner of its eye. It picked up Ash and flew off the perch.

Ash looked below. His stomach lurched. Pikachu and the others looked like tiny ants on the ground below.

"Char!" Behind him, Charizard roared angrily.

Ash couldn't believe it. "Charizard!" he shouted, "you evolved so you could rescue me. I thought you didn't want me as your trainer, but now I guess I was wrong."

Charizard roared. It shot a hot blast of

flame at Aerodactyl. The flame brushed against Ash's jeans.

"Ouch!" Ash yelled.

Charizard shot another blast of flame at the prehistoric Pokémon. Aerodactyl just barely dodged the blaze.

Suddenly, Ash realized the truth. Charizard didn't evolve to rescue him. It evolved to get revenge on Aerodactyl.

Even if it meant hurting Ash!

"Ouch!" Another blast of flame scorched Ash's jeans.

A wave of panic swept through Ash.

If Charizard won the battle, Ash would be toast.

And if Aerodactyl won the battle, Ash would be dinner.

Either way, Ash was the loser.

"Somebody help me!" Ash yelled.

8

Jigglypuff's Song

"Jigglypuff! Please sing your slumber song now," Misty pleaded.

Jigglypuff puffed up its round pink body. It hopped up on a rock and took out its microphone.

The Pokémon's strange melody began to fill the canyon.

"Jig-guh-lee-puff, jig-guh-lee-ee-ee-puff," it sang.

Misty felt her eyes grow heavy. Around her, Brock and the other fossil hunters looked tired, too.

Jigglypuff's song traveled high into the air. Ash could hear it. He felt sleepy . . . so sleepy.

Ash looked up at Aerodactyl. The Pokémon's eyelids were drooping.

"Hey, stay awake," Ash said sleepily. "If you fall asleep, we'll both fall . . ."

Ash drifted off to sleep.

Behind them, Charizard held its claws in its ears. It was protected from

Jigglypuff's song — for a little while. Now it flew after Aerodactyl with all its might.

Aerodactyl wobbled in the air. The Pokémon's wings flapped more and more slowly.

Jigglypuff's song was too strong for Aerodactyl. It closed its eyes. Its claws loosened their grip.

Ash fcll toward the ground!

Charizard zipped underneath Aerodactyl. Ash landed softly on the Fire Pokémon's back.

Below them, Aerodactyl plummeted to the ground.

The prehistoric Pokémon fell through the hole in the canyon floor. The ground shook. More rocks piled onto the hole.

Aerodactyl was sealed in the cave.

Charizard took its claws out of its ears. Jigglypuff's song was too strong for the Fire Pokémon, too. It landed gently on the ground. Ash rolled off its back and slept peacefully.

Jigglypuff looked out at its audience. Everyone was asleep!

The pink Pokémon puffed up its cheeks angrily. It made such beautiful music. Why did everyone always fall asleep when it sang? It just wasn't fair.

Jigglypuff picked up a black marker. It would show them. It would show them all for falling asleep.

While Ash and the others snored and dreamed, Jigglypuff drew on their faces with the marker.

Ash wasn't sure how long he was asleep. He woke up and looked around. His friends and the fossil hunters were waking up, too.

The police officer, Jenny, was making an announcement on a megaphone. A black eye and mustache were scribbled on her face with a black marker. "Some of you are claiming you saw a prehistoric Pokémon here in the canyon," she said. "That is ridiculous! Let me assure you it was only a dream caused by Jigglypuff's song."

A dream? Ash couldn't believe it. It was more like a nightmare.

"I have another announcement," Jenny continued. "Due to the danger of further cave collapses in the canyon, no more digging will be permitted."

"No more digging!" Ash

cried. It wasn't fair. Now he wouldn't get a chance to find a Pokémon fossil. He'd never beat Gary now.

Ash kicked at the dusty ground.

His foot struck something hard.

Ash bent down and brushed the sand away. Underneath was a large white egg. The egg was covered with red-and-blue triangles.

Ash picked up the egg and held it in his hands. The egg was heavy. It felt warm — like there might be something inside.

"Over here!" Ash called out. "I've found something over here."

Misty, Brock, and Pikachu ran up. They all had black marks on their faces from Jigglypuff's marker.

"Ash! You're all right!" Misty cried.

"Pikachu!" Pikachu hugged Ash.

"I'm better than all right," Ash said. He held out the egg. "Look what I found!"

Misty took the egg. She and Brock touched its smooth shell.

"I wonder what it is?" Brock asked.

The scientist from the fossil hunt

approached them. He looked at the egg through his thick glasses. He studied it carefully.

"This is no fossil," he said. "But I should congratulate you, young man. It seems you've found a very rare Pokémon egg!"

9

The Egg Hatches

"Did you hear that? I found a rare Pokémon egg!" Ash yelled.

A crowd of fossil hunters formed around Ash. He looked through the crowd and spotted Gary.

"Hey, Gary, what do you think of my egg?" Ash bragged. "It sure is better than what you dug up earlier."

Gary shrugged. "You got a lucky break, twerp. You've still got a long way to go before you become a better Pokémon trainer than me."

Gary stomped away. The other fossil hunters began to break up and leave the canyon. They were all still groggy from Jigglypuff's song.

Misty looked around the canyon. "Hey, I wonder where Jigglypuff is? I wanted to thank it for helping to save Ash."

"It was Jigglypuff *and* Charizard," Ash said. "They both saved me from Aerodactyl!"

"That Aerodactyl was one of a kind," Misty said. "It's too bad you couldn't capture it."

Brock frowned. "I don't know," he said. "I still think Aerodactyl would have been better off if we left it alone. I'm sure it's happier going back to sleep."

Ash shrugged. "I guess you're right. Besides, I don't need an Aerodactyl. I've got this rare egg, remember?" He reached out to take the egg from Misty. "I'd better start taking care of it right now."

Brock grabbed Ash's arm and stopped him. "Hold on there, Ash. What do you know about taking care of a rare Pokémon egg?"

"What do you mean?" Ash said.

"Well, you know you can be a little irresponsible sometimes," Brock said. "You could drop it or break it or something."

Ash glared at Brock. "So who *should* take care of the egg?"

"Well, me, of course," said Brock. "I'm the most experienced trainer. I would take the best care of it. It's common sense."

"That's not fair!" Ash said. "Just because you're older than me, you think —"

"Hey, guys," Misty interrupted, "I think you'd better stop arguing and watch this."

Ash and Brock turned. The egg was shaking in Misty's hands. Tiny bits of shell were breaking off.

"It's hatching!" Ash cried.

Two small white legs popped through the bottom of the shell. Next, two teeny white arms popped through the sides.

"This is amazing!" Brock said.

The top half of the shell began to crack. A tiny head poked out of the top of the shell.

The Pokémon had triangles sticking out of the top of its head. It had two cute black eyes and a triangle-shaped mouth.

"Toki," the Pokémon squeaked. It looked at Misty and smiled.

"It's so cute!" Misty said.

"Pika," Pikachu agreed.

Brock nodded. "It's very cute . . . but what is it?"

Ash took out his Pokédex. "Maybe Dexter knows."

"Togepi: an egg Pokémon," Dexter said. "Specific information about this Pokémon is still unavailable."

"Togepi! Even your name's cute," Misty said. She smiled at Togepi. The tiny Pokémon squeaked in delight.

Ash rolled his eyes. "Of course, it's cute. All babies are cute," he said. Ash took Togepi from Misty's arms. "And now I'll take my rare Pokémon, thank you."

"Hey!" Misty protested.

Ash looked at Togepi with pride. "I'll take care of you," he said.

Togepi's little smile turned into a frown. It began to cry softly.

"What'd I do?" Ash asked.

Brock took Togepi from Ash. "I knew you weren't ready to take care of something like this," Brock said. "I'll show you how it's done."

Brock held Togepi up to his face. "Hey there, little Pokémon."

Togepi only sobbed louder.

Misty took Togepi away from Brock. The tiny Pokémon immediately smiled and made happy sounds.

"Hey, what's going on?" Ash asked.

Dexter answered him. "Togepi is imprinted with the first thing it sees after it hatches, thinking this is its mother."

"That explains it," Brock said. "When it hatched, Misty was the first thing it saw."

"*Toki, toki,*" Togepi said happily.

"I knew it," Misty said. "Togepi likes me so much because it thinks I'm its mother."

Togepi flapped its tiny arms.

"Don't worry," Misty said, "I'll love you just like a mother would." She turned to

Pikachu. "You'll help me take care of Togepi, won't you?"

Pikachu smiled. *"Pika pi."*

Ash sighed. "Well, I guess it's the best thing for Togepi. I'll never have a rare Pokémon of my own, though, will I?"

Brock looked around the canyon. "Speaking of rare Pokémon, where's Team Rocket? I'm surprised they're not trying to steal Togepi."

Ash shrugged. "I'm sure they've blasted off to bug somebody else," he said. "Come on. Let's get out of this place and go find some more Pokémon!"

Ash and his friends walked off into the sunset. But in the cold cavern down below, Team Rocket was huddled together in fear.

They were trapped in the cave with the prehistoric Pokémon.

The Pokémon had all fallen into a deep sleep. Aerodactyl snored loudly. The Omanyte and Omastar were curled up in a corner. The Kabuto and Kabutops were sprawled out on the ground.

"What do we do now?" James whispered.

"Whatever we do, we should do it quietly," Jessie said.

"*Meowth!* How can Team Rocket blast off without making any noise?" Meowth asked.

"We'll find a way," Jessie promised. "And when we do . . ."

". . . we'll find that little pest, Ash," James said, "and we'll teach him a lesson once and for all!"

About the Author

Tracey West has been writing books for more than ten years. When she's not playing the blue version of the Pokémon game (she started with a Squirtle), she enjoys reading comic books, watching cartoons, and taking long walks in the woods (looking for wild Pokémon). She lives in a small town in New York with her family and pets.

Here's a sneak peek at...

POKÉMON #4

Night in the Haunted Tower

Ash spun around and ran across the gym. Misty and Brock were right behind him. They were almost through the open gym door.

Slam! The door flew shut.

"Sabrina used telekinesis to shut the door!" Brock cried.

Misty pounded on the door. "We're trapped!"

Sabrina's red eyes glared at them. In front of her, a man appeared out of nowhere.

The man grabbed Ash, Misty and Brock.

"Hold on tight!" he said.

Ash felt that familiar tingle. In a split second, they all teleported out of the gym. They reappeared outside on a street.

Ash looked up at the man. He had a scruffy beard. He wore a blue jacket and had a cap pulled low over his face.

"You teleported us out of there!" Ash said. "Why'd you help us?"

"That's not important," the man said gruffly. "What's important is that you're safe now. You should leave Saffron City before it's too late."

The man turned and began to walk away.

Ash rushed after him. "Wait!" he grabbed the man's sleeve.

"What is it?" the man asked.

"I can't leave Saffron City without getting

a Marsh Badge," Ash said. "You teleported us. You can tell me how to use telekinesis to beat Sabrina."

The man's eyes began to glow red. Ash felt his arms and legs begin to move. But he wasn't moving them! It was the man. The man made Ash fly through the air.

"See? You're powerless against telekinesis," the man growled. "You have to be born with these powers. You can't just learn them."

The red glow stopped. Ash could move his arms and legs again. The man turned and walked down the road.

Ash ran after him again. "There's got to be some way! Please! You've got to help me!"

The man sighed. "You don't give up, do you?" He paused. "There is one way. If you capture a Ghost Pokémon from Lavender Town, you might have a chance to defeat Sabrina!"

Ash grinned. "All right! I knew there was a way!"

The man shook his head. "What a foolish young man. No one has ever captured a

Ghost Pokémon from the haunted Pokémon Tower."

"Haunted tower? What do you—" Ash started, but before he could finish, the man disappeared.

"That was weird," Misty said. "I sure am ready to leave this place."

"Great!" Ash said. "'Cause we'd better head out for Lavender Town right away. It'll be dark in a few hours."

"Ash, are you crazy?" Misty asked. "You heard what he said about the haunted tower."

Ash didn't hear her. He was already running toward the gates of Saffron City.

Misty shook her head. "I guess we'd better follow him again."

"You're right," Brock agreed. "But I've got a strange feeling about this."

Hours later, Ash, Pikachu, Misty, and Brock were walking through the woods on the road to Lavender Town. A full moon was starting to rise over the trees. A thick gray fog surrounded them.

Brock led the way with a flashlight.

"Are we there yet?" Ash asked. "I can't wait to catch a ghost Pokémon. Then I'll beat Sabrina in no time."

"Ash, catching a Ghost Pokémon isn't easy," Brock said.

"Don't forget about the haunted tower," Misty said.

Ash laughed. "I'm not afraid of any—"

Ash stopped in his tracks. The trees parted in front of them. A round stone tower rose up into the night sky. Mist swirled around the tower's pointy roof. The doorway looked like a giant mouth with two eyes above it.

"So, Ash," Misty said. "Are you ready to enter the haunted tower?"

Catch It in October!

POKÉMON

now on video everywhere

$14⁹⁸ each

five volumes available:

I Choose You! Pikachu!

Mystery of Mt. Moon

Sisters of Cerulean City

Poké-Friends

Thunder Shock

POKÉMON
Poké-Friends

for more info see **WWW.PIONEERANIMATION.COM**